THE LEGENDS OF KING ARTHUR
MERLIN, MAGIC AND DRAGONS

Dados Internacionais de Catalogação na Publicação (CIP) de acordo com ISBD

M469f   Mayhew, Tracey
           The fall of Camelot / adaptado por Tracey Mayhew. – Jandira : W. Books, 2025.
           96 p. ; 12,8cm x 19,8cm. – (The legends of king Arthur)

           ISBN: 978-65-5294-171-8

           1. Literatura infantojuvenil. 2. Literatura Infantil. 3. Clássicos. 4. Literatura inglesa. 5. Lendas. 6. Folclore. 7. Mágica. 8. Cultura Popular. I. Título. II. Série.

2025-612   CDD 028.5
                                                                                        CDU 82-93

Elaborado por Vagner Rodolfo da Silva - CRB-8/9410
Índice para catálogo sistemático:
1. Literatura infantojuvenil 028.5
2. Literatura infantojuvenil 82-93

The Legends of King Arthur: Merlin, Magic, and Dragons
Text © Sweet Cherry Publishing Limited, 2020
Inside illustrations © Sweet Cherry Publishing Limited, 2020
Cover illustrations © Sweet Cherry Publishing Limited, 2020

Text by Tracey Mayhew
Illustrations by Mike Phillips

© 2025 edition:
Ciranda Cultural Editora e Distribuidora Ltda.

1st edition in 2025
www.cirandacultural.com.br
No part of this publication may be reproduced, stored in a retrieval system, or transmitted in any form or by any means, electronic, mechanical, photocopying, recording, or otherwise, without written permission of the publisher.
This book is a work of fiction. Names, characters, places, and incidents are either the product of the author's imagination or are used fictitiously, and any resemblance to actual persons, living or dead, business establishments, events, or locales is entirely coincidental.

THE LEGENDS OF KING ARTHUR

THE FALL OF CAMELOT

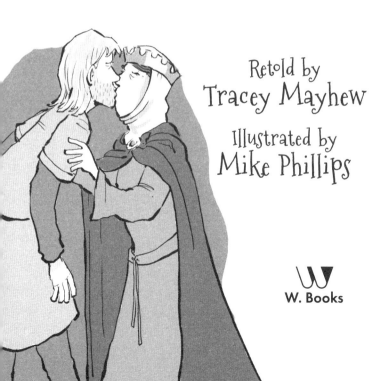

Retold by
Tracey Mayhew

Illustrated by
Mike Phillips

W. Books

Chapter One

King Arthur paced anxiously. His knights sat in silence at the Round Table, awaiting their orders. News that Guinevere had been kidnapped by King Meleagant, a supposed ally of Arthur's, had spread through Camelot like wildfire.

'How could this have happened?' Lancelot demanded. Like Arthur, he was unable to sit still.

'I don't know!' Arthur said, his frustration growing. 'Kay and his men were outnumbered.'

'But–'

'Enough!' Arthur snapped. 'When Meleagant's men approached them in the woods, Kay had no reason to expect betrayal.'

Lancelot clenched his jaw. Arthur was right. Meleagant's desire for Guinevere had been clear to everyone when he visited Camelot a few days ago, but no one had thought he would go this far.

Arthur continued in a low voice, 'I am just thankful that Kay managed to make it back to tell us what happened before he …'

Lancelot understood his king's despair: without Merlin, Kay's future was uncertain.

'I will lead the rescue party, Your Majesty,' Lancelot announced. He knew it was not his place to say so, but he could not help himself. Not when Guinevere was in danger.

Arthur met Lancelot's gaze. '*We* will lead it,' he corrected. Looking around the serious faces at the Round Table, he added, 'Half of our knights will remain here. The other half will travel with Lancelot and myself.' He turned to Gawain, sitting beside his two younger brothers, Sir Agravaine and Sir Gaheris. 'Gawain, you and your brothers will

stay here with Mordred, Bedivere and Griflet. You will protect Camelot and command those left behind.'

The knights bowed their heads in acknowledgment.

'We leave now. There is no time to lose,' Arthur announced. Then he strode from the chamber.

'We will find her,' Bors assured Lancelot as they rode out of Camelot.

'I pray you are right,' Lancelot replied.

Bors was the only person Lancelot had told about his love for Guinevere. Lancelot had confided it all to him one night, when Bors had mentioned seeing them together following Galahad's death. Queen Guinevere had appeared to be comforting Lancelot after his son had died.

Surprisingly, Bors had not condemned Lancelot for his feelings. He had also kept the knowledge to himself, for which Lancelot would be eternally grateful.

'For Queen Guinevere!' Arthur shouted from the head of their procession, raising his gauntleted fist in the air.

'For Queen Guinevere!' his men echoed as they marched in pursuit of King Meleagant.

Two days later, they reached Meleagant's castle: a tall, imposing fortress that left no doubt that this was where Guinevere was imprisoned.

Arthur gave instructions to hide their approach.

'There is no use trying to storm the castle,' he explained, under the cover of trees. 'We do not have the numbers to pierce their defences by force, and a siege would last too long. We need them to open the gates by choice so that we can get inside and find Guinevere.'

'But how?' asked Bors.

'We will send a messenger,' said Arthur. 'Once he is allowed inside, he will open the gate for us.'

'I volunteer!' said Lancelot, instantly.

Arthur took Lancelot aside to speak to him privately.

'We will come to your aid the moment they take you inside the castle. You must act quickly to overcome the guards and open the gate ready for us. Guinevere is all that matters. There is no one I trust more than you to help me save her.'

Lancelot nodded, feeling the familiar pang of guilt he always felt when Arthur said things like this.

They waited only long enough for the setting sun to give the rest of the men more cover in the shadowy hills. Then Lancelot rode forwards with his message. Two guards met him outside the gate.

Lancelot was not dressed as a knight, but as a messenger. He wore simple armour under a tunic with King Arthur's three-crown emblem on it. He carried a sword, but he made it seem as if he did not know how to use it. He fumbled to unbuckle it from his waist when ordered.

In the end he dropped it and the guards laughed.

'Look at this one!' one of them cried. 'The best Camelot has to offer, no doubt!'

Lancelot found himself pushed roughly through the gate before it dropped shut behind him.

There were more guards inside than had been visible when they'd planned this trick. One of them looked at Lancelot strangely.

'Isn't he—'

Before the man could finish speaking, Lancelot burst into action. He punched the guard closest to him, kicked dirt into the eyes of the next, retrieved his sword and sliced at a third. By the time he was done, men lay scattered around the courtyard, but few were seriously injured. Lancelot

knew that they would soon be on their feet again with more on the way. Quickly, he seized the pulley and tried to wrench the castle gate back up. It was too heavy.

'You!' He pointed his sword at the man who had recognised him earlier. He now had a gash across his temple. 'Pull the other chain.'

The guard was only young, and scrambled to obey. By the time they had opened the gate, Arthur and the other knights were surging through it. More of Maleagant's men arrived to meet them.

Lancelot pulled off his tunic so that he would not be recognised immediately as one of Arthur's men. Whilst the enemy focussed on the invading knights on horseback, Lancelot threatened the same young guard as before. 'Take me to Queen Guinevere or you will die here!'

Swallowing anxiously, the guard nodded. He led Lancelot towards the castle, against the tide of soldiers streaming towards the courtyard. Lancelot kept his sword hidden, but pressed it against the guard's back.

They went up a spiral staircase. At the top, two more guards stood outside a heavy wooden door. There was no point in pretending now. Lancelot knocked his prisoner unconscious and lunged at the guards. He killed them both.

Next Lancelot knelt and unhooked a set of keys from the belt of one of the dead men. He inserted one at a time into the lock, whilst the sound of fighting grew louder, came closer. He knew that it would not be long before reinforcements came to guard Guinevere.

Finally, the lock clicked. One of the keys had worked! Kicking the door open, Lancelot saw Guinevere cowering in the corner, a look of terror on her face.

'Lancelot!' she cried.

Lancelot ran to her, forgetting his duty as he embraced her.

'A touching reunion.'

Releasing Guinevere, Lancelot spun round. King Meleagant was standing in the doorway, sword in hand. He was older than Lancelot, and overweight. He would be all too easy to defeat. Lancelot only wished that Maleagant might live longer so that he could make him pay for what he had done.

Furiously, Lancelot swung his sword at Meleagant, Guinevere's sobs driving him on. Soon the other man began to tire and Lancelot, spotting an opening, drove his sword into his heart.

Meleagant was dead before he hit the ground.

Returning to Guinevere, Lancelot embraced her once more. 'You're safe now,' he whispered as she clung to him. 'You're safe …'

Chapter Two

The joy of Guinevere's safe rescue was overshadowed by the news that greeted them upon their return to Camelot: Kay was dead.

In the days following his brother's funeral, Arthur withdrew from his knights and his wife, spending each day alone in his chamber. For many months now he had been too busy to spend much time with Guinevere, but this was worse.

Finding herself even more alone than before, Guinevere struggled to return to normal life after her kidnapping. She was always uneasy, as if someone might be hiding around every corner just waiting to take her away again. Most nights she lay awake, listening to the noises of the castle, too afraid to sleep.

One day, as Guinevere made her way to the courtyard for some fresh air, she was glad to see Lancelot. At the sight of him, her heart felt lighter and she smiled for the first time in days.

Lancelot returned her smile and bowed. 'Good day, Your Majesty.'

'Good day, Lancelot. May I ask where you are going?'

'I am on my way to train the new recruits,' he replied.

'Perhaps I could join you some of the way?' she suggested hopefully. She was desperately in need of someone to talk to. Her lady's maid, Rowena, was good at her job, but she did like to gossip. Guinevere felt unable to confide in her about such sensitive feelings.

Lancelot's smile widened. 'Of course, Your Majesty. It would be my honour.'

Walking side by side, with Rowena following at a distance, neither of them was in any rush to reach their destination. For the first time since her kidnapping, Guinevere felt safe.

'How have you been these last few days?' Lancelot asked, glancing her way.

Guinevere hesitated. It would be so easy to pretend that everything was the same. That *she* was the same. But looking into Lancelot's eyes,

she knew that she could not lie to him. She told him everything that had happened during her kidnapping, and her fears since.

'I was so scared,' she concluded, wiping away a tear. 'I still am.'

Whilst Guinevere had poured her heart out to him, Lancelot had listened in silence. Inside, his emotions were not so quiet. He hated to hear her talk this way. He wanted nothing more than to hold her and tell her everything would get better. But he didn't. He couldn't.

Instead he promised, 'No one will ever make you feel like that again. You are safe here in Camelot, Your Majesty. Trust me.'

'I do trust you, Lancelot,' she said sincerely. 'And I thank you for rescuing me.'

Lancelot struggled not to let his feelings show. 'Any knight would have done the same,' he said gruffly. He stopped when they reached the path that led to the training ground. 'This is where I must leave you.'

'Very well. Thank you for listening.'

He bowed. 'It was my pleasure, Your Majesty. I hope

you will begin to feel better.'

'I'm sure I will.'

❦

The next few days continued like this: Guinevere and Lancelot would seek each other out and they would spend as long as possible talking. Guinevere did indeed begin to feel more like herself again.

Eventually, however, so did King Arthur. As Arthur's interest in life at Camelot returned, Lancelot and Guinevere suddenly found themselves spending less time together.

Guinevere felt the loss of Lancelot's company deeply and found herself longing to be with him, even though she knew that she should not. She believed that Lancelot felt the same way. She often caught him looking at her, though he would turn away as soon as their eyes met.

'Friends, we suffered a great loss,' Arthur announced one evening as everyone had sat down to feast. 'Kay's death cast a shadow over Camelot, but every cloud must pass! Kay will never be forgotten and tonight we will celebrate the life of a brave and honourable knight; a good friend and brother!'

A cheer went up as those gathered banged their cups on the tables.

Guinevere, sitting beside Arthur, glanced at Lancelot. She was pleased when he returned her smile.

'But we have another reason to celebrate,' Arthur continued. He

placed a hand on Guinevere's shoulder. 'Guinevere is back amongst us and I for one could not be happier, or more grateful to Lancelot for rescuing her!'

Another rousing cheer went up. Guinevere's gaze met Lancelot's once more, only this time neither of them smiled.

Later that night, Lancelot escaped the festivities. Leaning against the wall outside the doors of the Great Hall, with the hum of celebration in the background, he thought of Guinevere. Her kidnapping had rekindled every feeling he had tried for years to ignore, and spending so much time with her since had only made them stronger.

Lancelot looked up as the doors behind him opened. Guinevere stepped out.

'Your Majesty,' he greeted her.

'I saw you leave. Are you unwell?'

Lancelot smiled at her concern. 'I am fine. Just a headache.'

'Perhaps a walk would help,' she suggested.

'Perhaps it would.' He stepped forwards,

offering her his arm as they set off down the hallway.

'It's seems so long since we have walked together,' Guinevere said suddenly as they turned down an empty corridor. 'I have missed you.'

Her words pierced Lancelot's heart. 'I ...' He wanted to tell her how much he had missed her too. How much he hated them being apart. He wanted to confess his love. But how could he?

'Lancelot ...' Guinevere paused, looking away.

'What is it?'

Guinevere turned back to him. 'I must confess, my feelings towards you have deepened. I ...'

Lancelot could hardly breathe. Guinevere's eyes told him what neither of them could say. Without stopping to think of the treason he was committing, Lancelot leant forwards and kissed her.

Chapter Three

The tale of how Lancelot had saved Queen Guinevere was now a favourite at Camelot. Bors, in particular, delighted in adding details he had not been there to witness. Details of how Lancelot had single-handedly infiltrated Meleagant's castle before defeating Maleagant himself. It was a story that changed with each retelling.

In the Great Hall, Sir Mordred sat in silence as the rest of Camelot cheered their hero and Arthur hailed Lancelot the bravest of all men. Mordred glared, wondering just what Arthur's reaction would be if he were to discover Lancelot's affair with his wife.

Ever since Mordred had arrived at the castle aged sixteen, he and his mother, Morgan le Fay, had secretly sought every opportunity to destroy Camelot. So far their attempts had failed.

Until now.

Even before Guinevere had been kidnapped, Mordred had noticed the lovesick looks Lancelot had given her when he thought no one was looking. At first it had appeared that Lancelot's feelings were one-sided. But recently, since Guinevere's kidnap, it seemed that she loved him back.

The previous day, Mordred had ridden

from Camelot to inform his mother of his suspicions and she had told him that he needed proof of the affair. That was what he was waiting for now.

As Guinevere stood up and left the Great Hall, Mordred kept his eyes trained on Lancelot. It wasn't long before Lancelot rose, disappearing through the same door as Guinevere.

Mordred nodded to Sir Agravaine. Agravaine, too, suspected that the queen and Lancelot were having an affair, especially now that rumours had begun circling about secret meetings. These rumours were said to have started with the queen's own lady's maid. They also changed each time they were told.

Together, Mordred and Agravaine had recruited a small group of men who wanted to discover the truth for their king. It was this group of men who now followed Mordred after Lancelot.

Ducking into an alcove, Mordred signalled for the men to fall back. He held his breath when he heard Lancelot knocking on Guinevere's door. There

was a scrape as the door was unlocked. Mordred peered round the corner just as Lancelot disappeared inside the queen's bedchamber.

Together, Mordred, Agravaine and the others stepped out of the shadows. Mordred drew his sword as he led the way to Guinevere's door. Carefully, he lifted the latch, relieved to find that in his haste, Lancelot had not locked it behind him.

As Mordred threw the door open, Guinevere and Lancelot sprang apart. Guilt was written across their faces.

'Traitors!' Mordred cried, his sword already swinging. Lancelot, unarmed, was forced to step back,

taking Guinevere with him. Signalling to Agravaine, Mordred ordered, 'Seize her!' He sprang forwards, forcing Lancelot and Guinevere apart so that Agravaine could grab Guinevere's arms. Her terrified screams filled the air.

'Take your hands off her!' Lancelot

demanded, desperately trying to reach Guinevere.

Mordred held his sword to Lancelot's throat. 'Stay where you are.'

'Lancelot, my love, go!' Guinevere begged as tears streamed down her face. 'Save yourself!'

'Take her away!' Mordred ordered.

In the second that Mordred looked to see Guinevere being dragged away, Lancelot pulled his fist back and smashed it into Mordred's jaw. The younger knight sprawled onto the floor. Then Lancelot snatched his sword and thrust the blade towards the three men nearest to him. 'Come any closer and I will kill you all.'

'*Kill him!*' Mordred cried.

The men's hesitation was just what Lancelot needed. Backing up towards an open window, he turned and jumped.

Arthur was heartbroken. He sat upon his throne, looking down at his terrified wife as she cried on her knees for Lancelot. He had sent out men to track the traitor, but Lancelot had not been found. In fact, Sir Bors and Sir

Lionel had also disappeared, perhaps in support of their friend's betrayal.

Arthur's head pounded. He could feel everyone's eyes upon him, awaiting his verdict. He knew what he must do and yet–

'Your Majesty, by her own lips, she is a traitor,' Mordred pointed out, yet again. 'She has betrayed you in the worst possible way!'

Arthur gazed at Guinevere. She was still the woman he had fallen in love with. He continued to love her, despite her betrayal. Now, even more than when Kay had been mortally wounded, Arthur wished that Merlin were there to help him.

'The punishment for treason is clear!' Mordred continued. There were murmurs of agreement around him. 'You know what has to be done, Your Majesty.'

Arthur wished he could ignore what had happened. But if he let his wife go unpunished for a greater crime than others had died for, his people could riot. He could lose the respect of his court. His enemies could hear of his weakness and grow bolder in their attacks.

Camelot could fall.

Arthur had put his verdict off as long as he dared, half hoping that Guinevere would find a way to escape like her lover had. Now it was too late.

Hating himself, Arthur spoke the words: 'Guinevere, Queen of Britain, you have been found guilty of treason. I sentence you to death by fire!'

Chapter Four

The days following Guinevere's sentence were dark days indeed. Many in Camelot thought that Arthur had been too harsh in his punishment. This did not surprise Arthur, who knew how much the people loved her. As for Lancelot, he was their hero – perhaps even more than Arthur himself.

The day of Guinevere's execution dawned grey. Overhead, iron clouds gathered as if they, too, mourned for her. Arthur, Gawain and Mordred stood on the scaffold beside the pyre.

As Arthur surveyed the crowd, he placed his hand on Excalibur. Earlier that morning, he had discovered his scabbard missing, a fact that left him

vulnerable in battle. However, right now finding it was the last thing on his mind.

'Merlin foretold that this would happen,' he murmured.

'You *knew* this would happen?' Gawain demanded.

'Of course I didn't! But before he left, Merlin said that betrayal would come to Camelot.'

'Your Majesty, it is not too late,' Gawain murmured. 'You could still stop this.'

'And where does *your* loyalty lie?' Mordred sneered at him. 'With traitors or your king?'

Gawain glared at Mordred. 'There is no question: with our king, of course.'

'That's good to hear,' Mordred muttered as Bedivere approached Arthur.

'Your Majesty, it is time.'

Arthur nodded. Stepping to the edge of the scaffold, he raised his arms to silence the crowd. 'Today is a grave day,' he announced. 'A day I thought would never dawn in Camelot. Bring forth the prisoner!'

The crowd parted as Agravaine and Gaheris, unarmed and dressed in black robes, slowly made their way towards the pyre. Guinevere walked between them. She wore a plain white shift dress and looked only at

the ground. Her hair was tied back, revealing a pale face to the crowd. As she passed, some quietly offered up prayers. Others spat at her feet.

Suddenly, a shout split the air. A cloaked, hooded man ran out from the crowd in front of them. It was Lancelot.

Drawing his sword, Lancelot clashed with Agravaine. The younger knight did not stand a chance. Lancelot buried his blade in Agravaine's stomach, before tearing Guinevere from Gaheris's grasp. Gaheris lunged but Lancelot sliced his sword across his chest.

Screams tore through the air as chaos erupted.

Seeing his brothers fall, Gawain roared in fury and leapt from the scaffold. He forced his way through the panicked people in time to grip Gaheris's hand as he drew his last breath.

Closing his brothers' eyes, Gawain stood. Rage burned through him. It no longer mattered to him that

Lancelot had been his friend. He was ready to kill him for what he had done.

Pushing his way back through the panicking crowd, Gawain could barely see where he was going. Eventually, he spotted Arthur, Bedivere and Mordred.

'Where is he?' Gawain demanded.

Arthur took in Gawain's bloodstained hands. 'Are you hurt?'

'It is not my blood. Where is the traitor?' he demanded.

'He's gone. He escaped with Guinevere,' Arthur replied.

Bedivere looked grim. 'Many men left with him.'

'Who would follow him?' Gawain asked, disgusted. 'He killed my brothers in cold blood! They were unarmed!'

Arthur reached for Gawain's shoulder. 'You have my sympathy for your–'

'What I want is your *action*!' Gawain demanded, stepping out of reach. 'What are you going to do about this?'

Arthur sighed. 'Rally the men,' he said quietly. 'We are at war.'

Chapter Five

Dolorous Guard, the vast castle Arthur had gifted Lancelot many years ago, stood proudly on a clifftop overlooking the windswept sea. When Guinevere had first laid eyes on Lancelot's home,

she had loved it. Now, as she stood at her window looking down at the two camps below, she realised for the first time just what her love for Lancelot had cost. It was their actions alone that had brought about this war.

As for Gawain … she had witnessed Agravaine's and Gaheris's deaths and felt their loss as if they had been her own brothers. She knew that Gawain would never forgive them. She would never forgive herself, either.

The door behind her opened and Lancelot joined her. 'You wanted to see me, my love?'

'This war needs to end,' she said simply.

'I have given Arthur every opportunity to end it,' Lancelot reminded her. 'I never wanted this.'

'I know, my love, but you know why he fights, don't you?'

Lancelot hesitated. He knew the reason why Arthur would never surrender because it was the same as his. 'He loves you,' Lancelot replied.

A tear escaped as Guinevere nodded. 'I believe he still does, yes.'

'Then what do you want to do?'

Holding out a letter, Guinevere said, 'I have written this to Arthur.'

Lancelot scanned the words Guinevere now knew by heart. He could not believe them. 'You say you will return to him?'

Guinevere nodded. She stepped closer, taking his hand in hers. 'I will return to him if it brings an end to this madness. If it means no more innocent men dying in our names.' She gazed into his eyes. 'If it means *you* will not die.'

'But–'

'I have to do this, Lancelot.'

'Have you forgotten that he was about to execute you?' Lancelot demanded.

'We both know that he would not

have done so gladly. He is still Arthur. It is I who have changed, not he. Now I must try to make amends.'

The fight left Lancelot at her words. 'I don't like it,' was all he could say.

Guinevere smiled sadly. 'I never expected you to.'

Guinevere sent out a messenger to deliver the letter to Arthur. She and Lancelot waited anxiously for word that Arthur would meet with them, but nothing came. They were beginning to doubt if the letter had been a good idea when Guinevere's messenger returned, breathless.

'Sir!' he said to Lancelot. 'His Majesty, the king, wants to see you! He is waiting for you!'

Lancelot collected his horse and followed the messenger through the gatehouse to where Arthur waited, Bedivere and Mordred at his sides. They faced each other as enemies.

'I understand Guinevere is willing to return,' Arthur stated.

Lancelot nodded. 'She is. But only if you agree to do her no harm.'

Arthur shook his head sadly. 'I never wanted to harm her in the first place. It was *your* actions that led to that, Lancelot. Do not forget.'

Lancelot hung his head, guilt flooding him.

'Nevertheless,' Arthur continued, 'you have my word that I will never harm her.'

Looking up, Lancelot happened to catch the look on Mordred's face. It was clear that Mordred was against Arthur's decision.

'Do you agree?' Arthur asked. 'Will you let Guinevere go to bring an end to this war?'

For a moment, Lancelot considered saying no. Instead he nodded, and felt his heart break for the last time.

Chapter Six

'I am not leaving! Not until he has paid for what he did!'

Arthur tried desperately to make Gawain see sense. 'Killing Lancelot will not bring your brothers back.'

'Is that how you felt when he took Guinevere?'

Arthur paused. Gawain was right. He would have killed Lancelot for just taking Guinevere. It was only right that Gawain be allowed his chance to avenge the deaths of his brothers.

Arthur turned to Mordred, 'Accompany Guinevere back to Camelot.'

Mordred bowed. 'As you wish, Your Majesty.'

'Take thirty men with you.'

Bedivere stepped forwards. 'Your Majesty, should I–'

'No, I want you here, Bedivere. I may have need of you.' Arthur knew that when Gawain challenged Lancelot, it could easily spill into war again. He wanted to keep his best men around him.

'I hope you are ready for this,' he said to Gawain.

'I have never been more ready,' Gawain muttered.

The following day, Arthur and Bedivere could only stand and watch as Gawain paced outside Dolorous Guard, calling repeatedly for Lancelot to show himself. Arthur had never seen Gawain this angry. He was no longer the kind and chivalrous knight

Arthur had known for so long. Now he was filled with hatred and driven by vengeance.

'Lancelot, you coward!' he shouted. 'Come out and face me!'

Finally, movement at the gatehouse drew Arthur's eye. He watched as Lancelot, dressed in armour, walked slowly towards them.

Coming to a stop before Gawain, he reminded Arthur, 'We agreed the war was over.'

'This is between us!' Gawain spat. 'You killed my brothers. Now you pay!'

Lancelot was clearly reluctant to fight his old friend. 'Gawain, I am truly sorry for what I did. I will spend the rest of my life seeking forgive–'

Gawain slammed his helmet visor into place and launched himself at Lancelot. Lancelot defended quickly, but did not attack.

Gawain lunged again. 'Fight me!' he shouted.

Lancelot stifled a cry of pain as Gawain struck his sword arm. With no other choice, Lancelot lowered his stance and lifted his sword. The two men circled each other.

Gawain launched another attack. Then another. Lancelot deflected each blow easily. Gawain grew frustrated, and reckless. He pulled his helmet off. 'Fight me properly, you coward!'

'I won't fight you, Gawain!' Lancelot insisted.

Gawain charged furiously. Again, Lancelot only defended himself. But this time, Gawain was not wearing his helmet. Lancelot's blade caught Gawain on the head. Gawain dropped to the ground like a stone, blood pouring from the wound.

'It is done.'

Morgan le Fay looked up from the letter she had been writing. Mordred took the parchment, read it, and was amazed. Somehow, it was a letter in King Arthur's own handwriting, telling of a fatal wound he had suffered at the hand of the traitor Lancelot, and of his decision to hand Camelot over to Mordred.

None of it was true.

This was how Mordred and his mother were going to steal what was Arthur's from right under his nose. They were finally putting their plan into action.

Mordred smiled to himself as he caught sight of the scabbard lying on the table. Thanks to his mother's knowledge of its ability to prevent Arthur's death in battle, Mordred had used the chaos around Guinevere's affair as his chance to steal it. Next he would kill Arthur.

Morgan made her way to the window, surveying the scene outside. 'After all this time, Camelot will finally be ours.'

Chapter Seven

Gawain's death was slow. The injury was not terrible, but the infection that set in on the road back to Camelot was. They were forced to stop moving for Gawain's painful last days. Arthur stayed by his side until Gawain drew his last breath.

Arthur was eaten up by guilt. After all, if he had not sentenced Guinevere to death, or if he had only listened to Gawain and changed his mind …

'Your Majesty, a letter has come,' Bedivere said quietly.

Arthur left the last embers of Gawain's funeral pyre to take the scroll. He recognised Guinevere's handwriting. Quickly scanning the letter, his heart sank. 'Mordred has betrayed me! Guinevere says he has announced my death and my decision to leave Camelot to *him*! I cannot let this happen!'

'But what of Guinevere?' Bedivere asked.

'Mordred planned to marry her but she has escaped to a nunnery. She will remain there until I go to her. Order the men to ready themselves. We ride to meet Mordred immediately!'

Sitting astride his horse, Arthur gazed across the Camlann plain to where Mordred's army stood waiting. Even from this distance, Arthur could see Mordred clearly. His black cloak flapped in the breeze. Merlin had been right: betrayal had indeed come to Camelot. And it had arrived years ago.

It was obvious to Arthur that Mordred's men outnumbered his own. That meant that Mordred had been preparing for this for years. Arthur thought of the missing magical scabbard. He felt a tinge of fear as he considered that he could die in this battle. But then he thought of the men fighting for him, of Guinevere and Camelot, and he knew that he could not let Mordred win.

Across the plain, Arthur saw Mordred raise his arm and heard his battle cry. The armies surged towards each other, but Arthur's eyes stayed fixed on Mordred. They clashed loudly.

Arthur swung his sword, connecting with Mordred's shield just as Mordred struck his helmet. Arthur was stunned but he rallied, turning his horse and swinging again. They continued like that, horses dancing, swords flashing. Occasionally, in the chaos, they were

forced to fight other enemies, but they always returned to fighting each other. Eventually, Mordred was thrown from his horse and Arthur's was cut down underneath him. They continued fighting on foot.

Arthur leapt forwards, stabbing at Mordred, before immediately spinning and hitting him on the back of his helmet with his sword pommel. The younger man stumbled.

Mordred launched a series of attacks. Arthur caught each blow with his shield, until the shield itself began to break. When it was useless, Arthur threw it aside and scrambled for another amongst the bodies of fallen men. Mordred seized his chance. Stepping forwards, he thrust his sword into Arthur's stomach.

Time stood still as the two men looked at each other, then Arthur dropped to his knees. With the strength he had left, Arthur lifted Excalibur and drove it up into Mordred's chest.

Arthur watched as Mordred fell

to the ground, his sightless eyes staring back at him.

Immediately, the earth began to shake. Thunder rumbled and lightning split the sky. Morgan le Fay appeared out of nowhere, her robes billowing around her.

'My son!' she screamed, dropping to her knees beside Mordred. She glared at Arthur. 'You will pay for this!' Sparks of lightning intensified at her fingertips as she stood and drew her arm back …

Suddenly, she gasped. Her mouth and eyes grew wide with shock. She looked down at the sword that had burst through her chest. It disappeared as it was pulled free, then Morgan fell beside her son. Bedivere stood behind her, the bloodied sword in his hand.

Intense relief filled Arthur. Then the world went black.

'Your Majesty!'

Arthur blinked awake. An exhausted, bloodstained Bedivere was staring down at him. Behind Bedivere, Arthur's surviving men knelt with their heads bowed respectfully.

'Mordred?' he gasped.

'Dead, Your Majesty. You defeated him.'

'And Morgan?'

'Also dead,' Bedivere replied.

The news brought Arthur no joy. He had wanted none of this. He gazed down at his wound. It was fatal.

'It is too late for me, Bedivere. Take Excalibur–'

'Your Majesty, I cannot. Excalibur is yours.'

Arthur swallowed. 'You must return it to the lake. You know the one I speak of?'

Bedivere had heard many stories of how Arthur had got Excalibur. As usual, none had contained the whole truth.

He nodded.

Arthur coughed and struggled to speak. 'Take Excalibur and throw it into the lake.'

'Throw–? But Sire!'

'Please, do this last thing I ask. The lake not far from here. Ride west and you will find it. Return when it is done.'

Nodding, Bedivere took Excalibur. He mounted the nearest horse and rode quickly to the lake. But when he got there, he gazed at the beautiful sword and could not bring himself to throw such a weapon away. He hid it in some long grass, promising to return later to retrieve it.

Riding back to Arthur, Bedivere told the king that he had done as he had asked.

'What did you see?' Arthur asked, struggling to keep his eyes open.

Bedivere shrugged. 'Nothing. The sword sank into the water.'

This angered Arthur. 'Lies! Bedivere, I command you to throw Excalibur into the lake!'

Not understanding how his king knew what had happened, but determined to carry out his wishes, Bedivere rode back to the water. He retrieved Excalibur and this time threw it with all his might into the lake. Before it landed in the very centre, a slender hand reached out the water. It caught the sword easily, before lowering it, inch by inch, back into the lake it had come from.

Upon his return, Bedivere recounted what he had witnessed at the lake.

'Thank you, my friend,' Arthur murmured. 'That was the Lady of the Lake.'

Then Arthur, the greatest King of Britain, closed his eyes and died.

Or so this story goes. There are other stories that say he will rise again. Still others that say he never died at all. That Arthur was taken to the enchanted isle of Avalon to heal after his battle with Mordred. And that one day, when Britain needs him most, King Arthur will return.

"This series opens the door to a treasure house of wonderful stories which have previously been available chiefly to older readers. We can only welcome it as a fabulous resource for all who love magical tales, and those who will come to love them."

JOHN MATTHEWS
AUTHOR OF THE RED DRAGON RISING SERIES AND ARTHUR OF ALBION